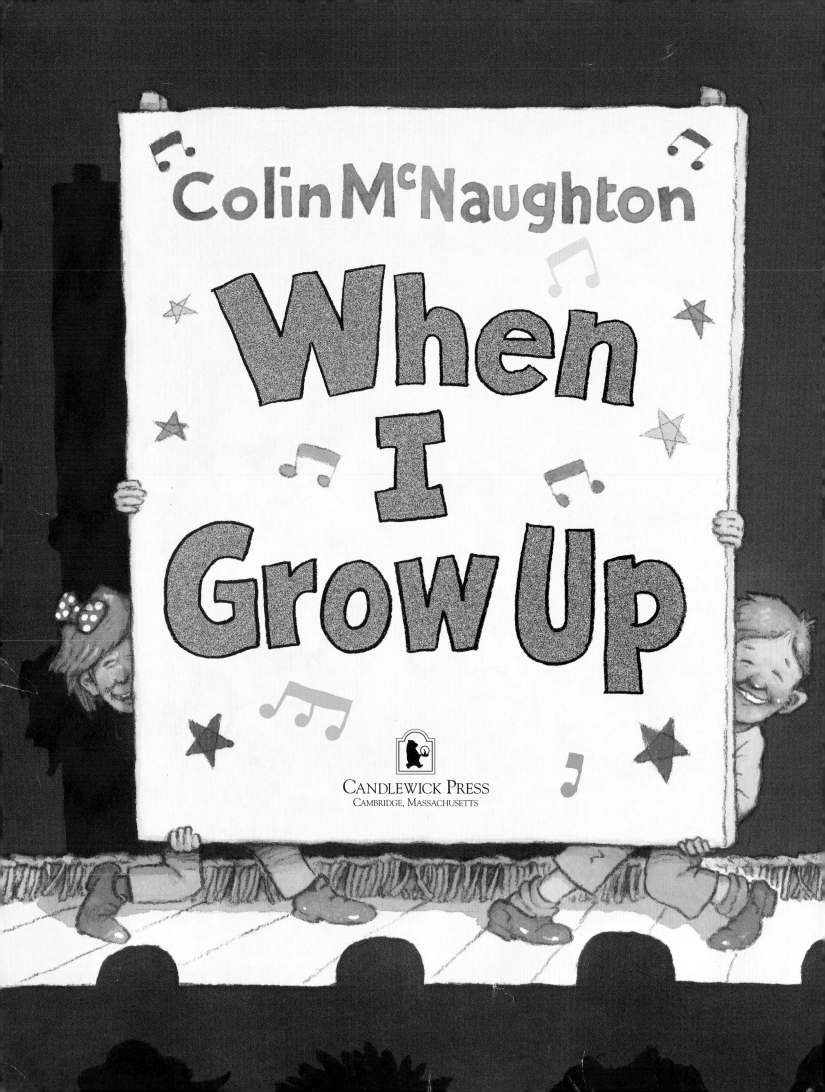

Colin McNaughton

When I Grow Up

CANDLEWICK PRESS
CAMBRIDGE, MASSACHUSETTS

"Ladies and gentlemen, welcome along to a musical packed with action and song. Sit back in your seats; we're ready to go. So strike up the band and it's on with the show!"

"When I grow up,
I'd like to be
An explorer
of the galaxy."

"When I grow up,
I'd like to be
King of the jungle—

wheee

Be careful, Colin!

"**W**hen I grow up—
well, I just know it—
I'll become
a famous poet."

"When I grow up,
I'd like to be
An angel
oh so heavenly."

"**W**hen I grow up,
well, bless my soul,
I'll be the king
of rock 'n' roll!"

"**W**hen I grow up,
I'd like to be
Just like my dad
and go to sea."

That's
my girl!

"When I grow up,
I'd like to be
Married with
a family."

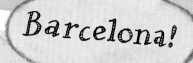

"When we grow up,
it's our dream
To join our favorite
soccer team."

"When we grow up,
me and Joan,
We'd like a sweet shop
of our own."

"When I grow up, I'd like to be

Rich and famous on TV."

"When I grow up,
I'd like to be

Called
'Your Royal Majesty.'"

"When I grow up,
I'd like to be
A mermaid in
the deep blue sea."

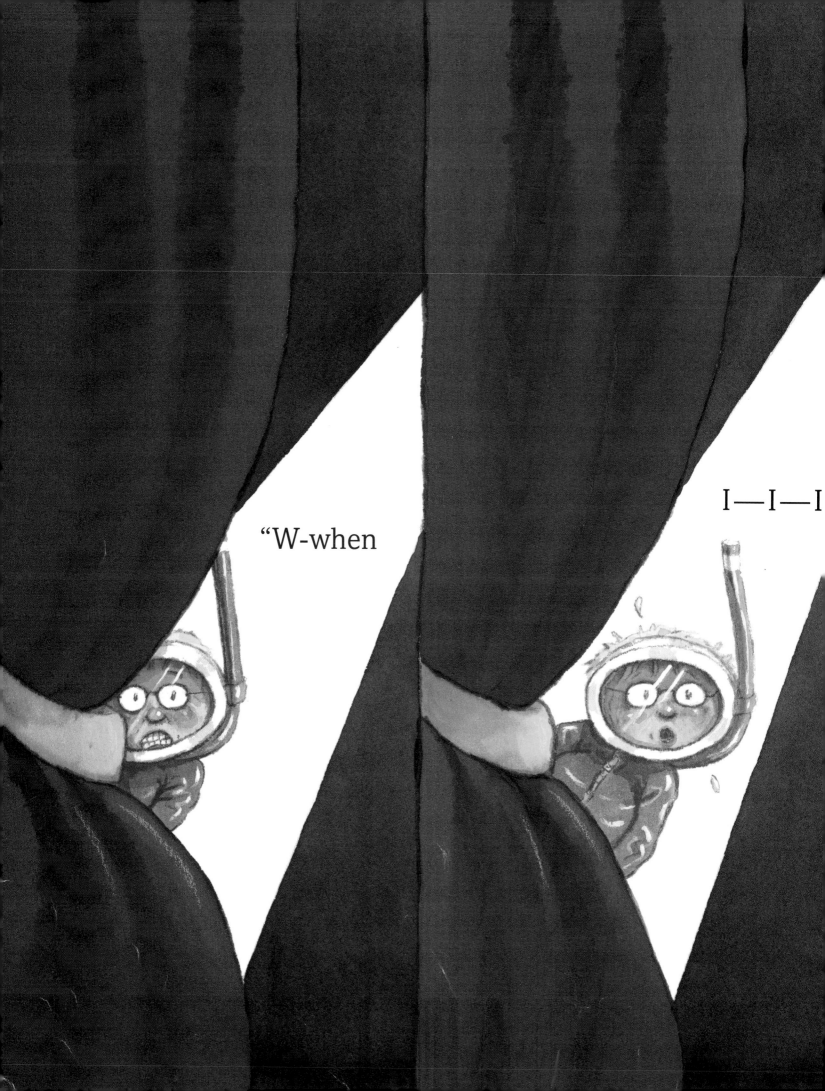

"W-when   I—I—I

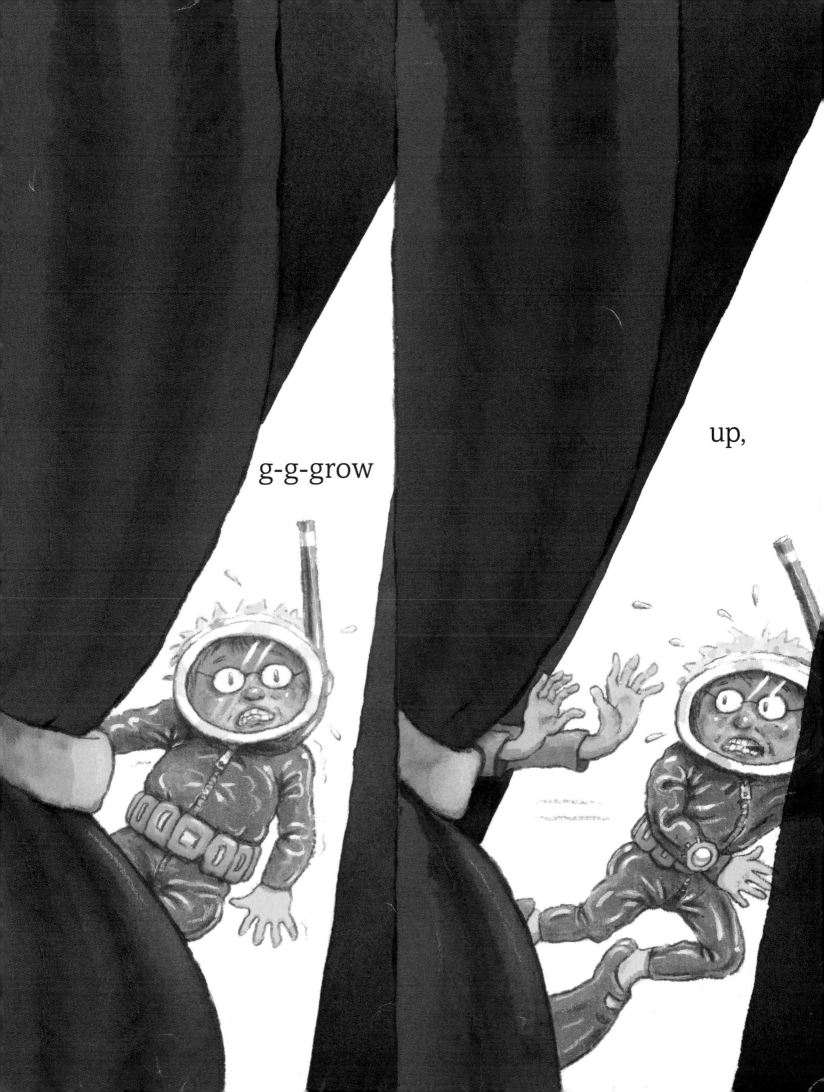

AH!

"I don't wanna grow up!"

"There, there, sweetheart,
don't you fret.
You don't have to
grow up *yet*.
(I know *lots* of
grownups who
Still don't know
what they want to do.)

Enjoy your childhood
while you may—
Growing up is
years away!"

sniff...